WARRIORS

TIGERSTAR & SASHA

#3: RETURN TO
THE CLANS

WARRIORS
TIGERSTAR & SASHA

#3: RETURN TO
THE CLANS

CREATED BY
ERIN HUNTER

WRITTEN BY
DAN JOLLEY

ART BY
DON HUDSON

HAMBURG // LONDON // LOS ANGELES // TOKYO

HarperCollins*Publishers*

Warriors: Tigerstar and Sasha Vol. 3:
Return to the Clans
Created by Erin Hunter
Written by Dan Jolley
Art by Don Hudson

Cover Colorist - Jason Van Winkle
Digital Tones - Lincy Chan
Lettering - John Hunt
Production Artist - Michael Paolilli
Cover Design - Tina Corrales

Editor - Lillian Diaz-Przybyl
Print Production Manager - Lucas Rivera
Managing Editor - Vy Nguyen
Senior Designer - Louis Csontos
Associate Publisher - Marco F. Pavia
President and C.O.O. - John Parker
C.E.O. and Chief Creative Officer - Stu Levy

A  Manga

TOKYOPOP and ⊙ are trademarks or registered trademarks of TOKYOPOP Inc.

TOKYOPOP Inc.
5900 Wilshire Blvd. Suite 2000
Los Angeles, CA 90036

E-mail: info@TOKYOPOP.com
Come visit us online at www.TOKYOPOP.com

Text copyright © 2009 by Working Partners Limited
Art copyright © 2009 by TOKYOPOP Inc. and HarperCollins Publishers
All rights reserved. Printed in the United States of America.
No part of this book may be used or reproduced in any manner whatsoever without written permission
except in the case of brief quotations embodied in critical articles and reviews.
This manga is a work of fiction. Any resemblance to actual events or locales or persons,
living or dead, is entirely coincidental.
For information address HarperCollins Children's Books, a division of HarperCollins Publishers,
10 East 53rd Street, New York, NY 10022.
www.harpercollinschildrens.com

ISBN 978-0-06-154794-2
Library of Congress catalog card number: 2008908581

11   12   13   LP/BVG   10   9   8   7   6   5   4
❖
First Edition

Hello again!

When Sasha returns to the forest with her kits, she is terrified that they'll be seized by a ShadowClan patrol until an unexpected friend brings startling news: Tigerstar is dead. When we watched Tigerstar lose his nine lives in *The Darkest Hour*, I wanted us to feel something much more complicated than straightforward relief that Firestar's number one enemy had been vanquished. Instead, I wanted us to share Firestar's shock and even grief that a brave, skillful warrior had been killed just when the Clans needed all their best fighters.

Sasha is going to have a similar response to news of Tigerstar's demise. Her kits may be safe from being snatched by the cruel, ambitious leader of ShadowClan—but at the same time, they have lost their father, who would have shared Sasha's pride in them as she watches them grow up. Sasha is smart enough—and forgiving enough—to recognize the strength in the way the Clans live. She's a truly remarkable cat, one who has experienced life as a kittypet, a Clan cat, and now a loner, and been able to see the value in each of these. I think we know where Sasha has been happiest, but what about her kits? Which life will she choose for them?

Walk this way, to a windswept forest, and find out. . . .

Best wishes always,
Erin Hunter

THESE KITS ARE MY WHOLE LIFE NOW. BUT...HAVE I DONE THE RIGHT THING? I'M SO COLD, AND TIRED...

AM I JUST BEING SELFISH, WANTING TO RAISE THEM IN THE WOODS?

I'VE NAMED THEM WELL, I THINK.

HAWK...

...HIS SISTER MOTH...

...AND THE OLDEST, TADPOLE.

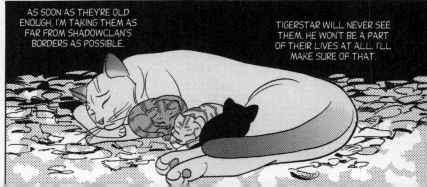

AS SOON AS THEY'RE OLD ENOUGH, I'M TAKING THEM AS FAR FROM SHADOWCLAN'S BORDERS AS POSSIBLE.

TIGERSTAR WILL NEVER SEE THEM. HE WON'T BE A PART OF THEIR LIVES AT ALL. I'LL MAKE SURE OF THAT.

BUT I STILL WISH THEY COULD SEE HOW STRONG THEIR FATHER IS...HOW COMMANDING...

...HOW WONDERFUL HE CAN BE.

I WON'T SEE HIM, NOT EVER AGAIN, NOT WHEN I'M AWAKE. BUT, MORE NIGHTS THAN NOT...

...I SEE HIM IN MY DREAMS.

EVEN THERE, I CAN'T BEAR TO TALK TO HIM. NOT AFTER WHAT I LEARNED ABOUT HIM, ABOUT HIS TRUE NATURE.

I KNOW IT'S ONLY A DREAM. ...BUT IT STILL HURTS.

THE KITS STAY IN THE DEN, OF COURSE, WHILE I HUNT. AND AS SCRAWNY AND WEAK AS I'VE GOTTEN...

...MOST DAYS IT'S A RELIEF THAT THEY CAN'T SEE ME. I'D BE SO EMBARRASSED.

I NEVER GIVE UP, THOUGH. NEVER EVEN CONSIDER IT. AND IF WHAT I FINALLY BRING HOME IS A PITIFUL LITTLE MOUSE...

...WELL, THAT'S JUST FINE.

THE SUN RISES AND SETS, RISES AND SETS...AND FINALLY...TOWARD THE END OF LEAF-BARE...

...I GET MY STRENGTH BACK.

C'MERE, YOU BUSHY-TAILED MORSEL...!

NO POINT IN RUNNING...

...YOU'RE JUST DELAYING THE INEVIT—

NO...NO! I CAN'T FACE TIGERSTAR! AND THAT GINGER CAT—RUSSETFUR.

SHE KNOWS ME! SHE'S GOING TO TELL EVERYONE WHO I AM!

HMMM.

I THINK NOT. WHOEVER SHE IS, SHE'S TOO SCRAWNY TO BE ANY KIND OF THREAT. AND BLOODCLAN CATS ARE BETTER FED.

I SAY WE LET HER GO...IF SHE AGREES NOT TO COME BACK.

I CAN'T BELIEVE IT! SHE'S HELPING ME! I'M GOING TO GET OUT OF THIS ALIVE AFTER ALL...!

WAIT, WAIT, WAIT.

snff snff

I SMELL MILK ON HER.

SHE MUST HAVE KITS CLOSE BY!

13

OH, PLEASE, NO, DON'T...IF THEY FIND MY KITS, THEY'LL STEAL THEM, AND FORCE THEM TO BE SHADOWCLAN WARRIORS!

ESPECIALLY IF TIGERSTAR FINDS OUT THEY'RE HIS...!

I...I DID. I DID HAVE KITS.

THE COLD WAS...TOO MUCH FOR THEM.

THEY ALL DIED.

HOW HORRIBLE...!

YOU POOR THING. LISTEN...YOU CAN GO BACK WHERE YOU CAME FROM.

GO ON, NOW.

I CAN BARELY BREATHE, MY HEART'S BEATING SO FAST, BUT I TRY NOT TO LET IT SHOW.

AT LEAST NOT SO THE KITS CAN SEE.

MY CLOSE CALL MAKES ME FEEL A BIT GENEROUS. I DECIDE TO LET MY KITTENS COME OUT AND PLAY...

...A TREAT THEY DON'T GET OFTEN ENOUGH.

WE'RE FINALLY OUT OF THE DEN! COME ON, COME ON!

ARE YOU SURE IT'S SAFE, TADPOLE? WHAT ABOUT...

...WHAT ABOUT FOXES?

DON'T WORRY, MOTH! I WON'T LET ANY STUPID FOXES HURT YOU!

OKAY! I'LL FOLLOW YOU! ...UH, WHERE ARE WE GOING?

WHAT HAPPENED TO KEN?

I DON'T KNOW.

ONE DAY HE WAS THERE. THE NEXT DAY HE WAS GONE.

AND I NEVER FOUND OUT WHERE HE WENT.

OR WHY.

DON'T BE SAD, MAMA.

I CAN'T LET MYSELF THINK ABOUT KEN TOO MUCH. I HAVE MY OWN KITS TO LOOK AFTER NOW.

AND THEY NEED ME JUST AS MUCH AS I NEEDED KEN AND JEAN. MAYBE EVEN MORE.

I'LL TAKE GOOD CARE OF THEM. NO MATTER WHAT. THEY'RE ALL I HAVE.

AND TIGERSTAR WILL NEVER GET HIS PAWS ON THEM. NO MATTER HOW OFTEN HE INVADES MY DREAMS.

DON'T WORRY.

AS SOON AS THEY'RE STRONG ENOUGH TO TRAVEL, WE'RE ALL LEAVING THIS PART OF THE FOREST FOR GOOD.

ALL RIGHT.

I SHOULD GO.

YOU HAVE A LOVELY FAMILY, SASHA.

I HOPE THEY GROW UP STRONG AND HEALTHY.

I'M SADDER THAN I EXPECTED TO BE, WATCHING RUSSETFUR WALK AWAY. I WISH WE COULD'VE KNOWN EACH OTHER...

...IN BETTER TIMES.

TIGERSTAR'S DEATH HURTS ME. IT FEELS AS IF A PART OF ME JUST DIED WITH HIM. AND YET...I'M RELIEVED, TOO.

I DON'T HAVE TO LIE TO MYSELF ANYMORE. PRETEND I DIDN'T LOVE HIM WITH ALL MY HEART. THAT WAS SO HARD...

AND NOW I CAN JUST REMEMBER.

REMEMBER HOW KIND AND BRAVE HE WAS, AND HOW MUCH HE TAUGHT ME.

OH, TIGERSTAR...

...I'LL MISS YOU.

ALWAYS.

THAT NIGHT, WHEN I FINALLY SLEEP, I TRY TO SPEAK TO TIGERSTAR IN MY DREAM...

...BUT HE LEAVES ME.

I DON'T KNOW WHAT IT MEANS.

...I WISH HE'D STAY.

THE KITS DON'T KNOW ANYTHING ABOUT THEIR FATHER, OF COURSE.

I THINK ABOUT TELLING THEM. CONSTANTLY I THINK ABOUT IT.

BUT THE TIME NEVER SEEMS RIGHT.

INSTEAD I CONTENT MYSELF WITH WATCHING THEM GROW.

THEY'RE SO PERFECT.

I TRY MY BEST NOT TO LET THEM KNOW HOW HARD THINGS ARE RIGHT NOW.

FOOD IS SCARCE DURING LEAF-BARE, AND HALF THE TIME WHEN I FINALLY FIND SOME, I HAVE TO FIGHT FOR IT.

SEEMS AS IF I HAVE TO GO FARTHER AND FARTHER AWAY FROM THE DEN EACH TIME I GO HUNTING, TOO.

IT CAN'T BE HELPED, THOUGH. I HAVE TO KEEP AS MUCH DISTANCE AS POSSIBLE BETWEEN ME AND SHADOWCLAN...

...AND THAT PUTS A HUGE SECTION OF THE FOREST OFF-LIMITS.

OKAY...SHE'S GOING...SHE JUST LOOKED BACK, LIKE SHE ALWAYS DOES... ANNND...

...SHE'S IN THE TREES!

LET'S GO!

33

THEY'RE CALLED "CARS," BUT DON'T WORRY. THEY STAY ON THOSE BIG PATHS. MOST OF THE TIME, ANYWAY.

LISTEN, YOU LOOK A LITTLE LOST. WHY DON'T YOU COME OVER HERE, WHERE IT'S SAFE? THERE'S PLENTY OF ROOM IN MY YARD.

HE SEEMS NICE. MAYBE HE KNOWS WHERE KEN IS!

WAIT, WAIT, HOLD ON! DIDN'T MAMA TELL US NEVER EVER EVER TALK TO STRANGERS?

WHAT'S A YARD? LET'S GO SEE!

WELL.... YEAH...

THANKS, BUT WE KNOW EXACTLY WHERE WE'RE GOING.

RIGHT. SO WE DON'T NEED YOUR YARD.

"WE HAVE IMPORTANT PLACES TO GO."

NAPTIME'S OVER, KITLINGS. MAMA'S GOT A NICE BIRD FOR Y—

KITS?

NO SHADOWCLAN.

NO FOX. NO BADGER, NO DOG.

OH, PLEASE, PLEASE PLEASE, LET THEM BE OKAY.

SASHA? IS THAT YOU?

SHNUKY! YOU STARTLED ME!

SORRY.

I DIDN'T THINK YOU WERE COMING BACK! WEREN'T YOU DONE WITH THIS PLACE?

I AM, BUT... IT'S MY KITS. THEY RAN OFF THIS MORNING. I'M ON THEIR TRAIL, AND IT LEADS HERE.

OOHH...ALL RIGHT, THAT MAKES A LITTLE MORE SENSE NOW. I DID SEE THREE KITS HERE EARLIER.

THEY SAID THEY HAD IMPORTANT PLACES TO GO, AND RAN OFF!

"IMPORTANT PLACES..." THEY'LL BE LUCKY IF THEY DON'T RUN IN FRONT OF A CAR...!

WOULD YOU, MAYBE, LIKE SOME HELP LOOKING FOR YOUR LITTLE ONES?

COME ON, YOU TWO. I THINK IT'S THIS WAY.

TADPOLE, THIS IS HOPELESS! WE DON'T EVEN KNOW WHICH OF THESE DENS HE LIVED IN!

CAN WE GO HOME SOON? I THINK IT'S GONNA RAIN.

LOOK, WE'VE ALL HEARD MAMA TALK ABOUT THE PLACE SHE USED TO LIVE. I'M SURE WE'LL KNOW IT WHEN WE—

WHERE DO YOU LITTLE SCRAPS THINK YOU'RE GOIN'?

—UH, WHEN WE SEE IT...

STRANGERS AREN'T WELCOME AROUND HERE!

AND...IS THAT... FOREST I SMELL ON YOU?

THREE LITTLE SCRAPS, STRAIGHT FROM THE WOODS...

YOU BETTER TELL ME WHAT YOU'RE DOING HERE, ALL THREE OF YOU. AND MAKE IT QUICK!

WHAT IS THIS PLACE? WHAT'RE ALL THOSE THINGS?

IT'S ALL TWOLEG STUFF. IT'S GOTTA BE.

C'MON, WE CAN EXPLORE AND HUNT! IT'LL BE AN ADVENTURE!

SEE? THERE'S OUR DINNER! GET IT!

WAIT FOR ME, TADPOLE! I'M COMING TOO!

42

"TADPOLE?"

YEAH?

I'M SORRY WE DIDN'T CATCH THE MOUSE.

IT'S ALL RIGHT. I DON'T THINK WE'RE GOING TO GET ANYTHING TO EAT IN HERE, THOUGH. IT'S PROBABLY SAFE TO LEAVE BY NOW.

HEY! THAT THING WE CAME THROUGH--IT'S SHUT!

HOW'RE WE GONNA GET OUT OF HERE?

DON'T WORRY, DON'T WORRY. I'LL TAKE A LOOK AT IT.

IT'S STUCK. I CAN'T... CAN'T SEEM TO GET IT...TO MOVE.

WHAT DO WE DO?

WE'RE TRAPPED IN HERE!

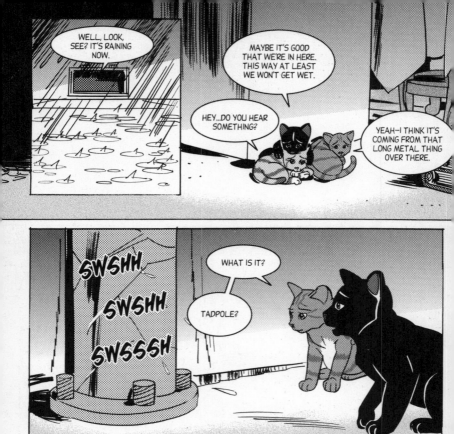

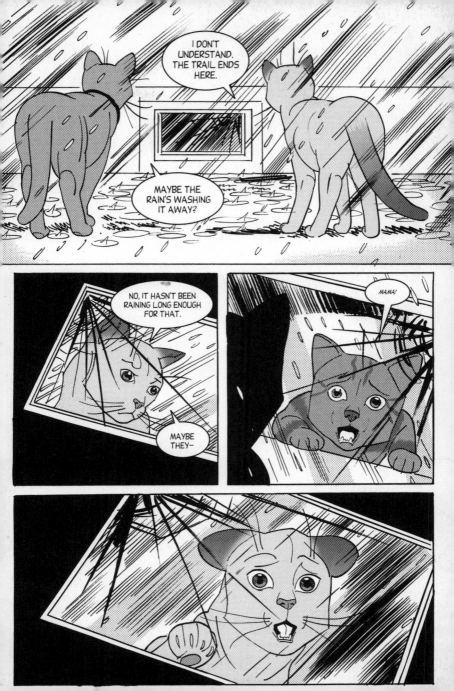

AND IT'S ON THE FAR SIDE OF THE RIVER, SO YOU WON'T HAVE SO MUCH TROUBLE FINDING FOOD!

...BUT I JUST HAD THE BEST IDEA! LISTEN, THERE'S THIS FARM! I KNOW THE CATS THERE, THEY'RE REALLY FRIENDLY.

I CAN TAKE YOU THERE! ALL OF YOU! WHAT DO YOU SAY?

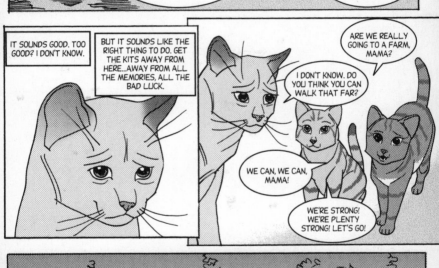

IT SOUNDS GOOD. TOO GOOD? I DON'T KNOW.

BUT IT SOUNDS LIKE THE RIGHT THING TO DO. GET THE KITS AWAY FROM HERE...AWAY FROM ALL THE MEMORIES, ALL THE BAD LUCK.

ARE WE REALLY GOING TO A FARM, MAMA?

I DON'T KNOW. DO YOU THINK YOU CAN WALK THAT FAR?

WE CAN, WE CAN, MAMA!

WE'RE STRONG! WE'RE PLENTY STRONG! LET'S GO!

WELL, IT SOUNDS AS IF THE DECISION'S BEEN MADE.

THANK YOU, PINE. I OWE YOU A LOT FOR THIS.

HE'S RIGHT. IT IS BEAUTIFUL.

HEY, IT'S PINE!

GOOD TO SEE YOU, PINE!

AND THE CATS DO LOOK VERY HEALTHY HERE.

BUT IMMEDIATELY I GET THE SENSE THAT PINE'S PERFECT FARM IS FAR TOO GOOD TO BE TRUE.

AT LEAST FOR MY KITS AND ME.

ALL RIGHT. NOW THAT PINE'S GONE...IT'S TIME TO GET A FEW THINGS STRAIGHT.

LOOK, WE DON'T WANT ANY TROUBLE...

OH, YOU DON'T WANT ANY TROUBLE? WELL, IT'S TOO LATE FOR THAT.

WE RESPECT PINE. WE'VE KNOWN HIM FOR A LONG TIME. BUT YOU AND YOUR FLEA-BITTEN BROOD?

WE DON'T PUT UP WITH YOUR KIND AROUND HERE. LOOK AT YOU. YOU'RE A DISGRACE. FILTHY, HOMELESS ROGUES.

AS IF WE'D SHARE OUR HUNTING GROUNDS WITH YOU. WE WANT YOU GONE.

AND JUST TO MAKE SURE YOU DON'T COME BACK...

RAOWW! MY EAR!

YOU CUT MY EAR!

MY KITS AND I ARE GOING TO LEAVE AN IMPRESSION FIRST.

HEY!

SEE, MY KITS ARE STRONG. HEALTHY.

TOO BAD YOU WON'T BE STAYING. YOU COULD LEARN A FEW THINGS ABOUT MOTHERHOOD.

BESIDES.

I'VE JUST GIVEN HER A LIFETIME'S WORTH OF HUMILIATION.

YOU'RE...YOU'RE ONE OF THOSE STUPID WARRIORS, AREN'T YOU?

HER QUESTION TAKES ME OFF-GUARD. FOR A FEW HEARTBEATS I'M...I'M NOT SURE.

WARRIORS...AM I A WARRIOR? MY KITS ARE HALFCLAN, BUT... WHAT AM I?

BUT THEN...THEN MY TIME IN SHADOWCLAN COMES BACK TO ME. AND I KNOW.

THAT'S RIGHT.

I AM A WARRIOR.

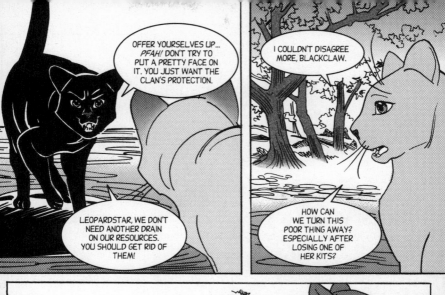

...OR JUST ANOTHER STOP?

EVEN THOUGH IT DOESN'T LOOK THE SAME, THIS PLACE REMINDS ME SO MUCH OF SHADOWCLAN.

IS THAT A GOOD THING? I HOPE SO.

SASHA. HAWK. MOTH.

WELCOME TO RIVERCLAN!

IT'S A LITTLE LIKE A WHIRLWIND, ALL THE NEW CATS, ALL THE NEW NAMES.

FIRST IS RIVERCLAN'S MEDICINE CAT, MUDFUR.

NASTY LITTLE RIP YOU HAVE THERE, HAWK.

IT DOESN'T HURT. I'M TOUGH. I'M NOT SCARED!

NEVER THOUGHT YOU WERE SCARED. WE STILL NEED TO GET IT HEALED, THOUGH, IF YOU'RE GOING TO BE A WARRIOR. RIGHT?

KEEP THIS COBWEB ON IT...AND I'LL GET YOU ALL SOME POPPY SEEDS TO HELP YOU SLEEP.

NEXT STOP, THE NURSERY. THE ONE STORMFUR TALKED ABOUT BEING NEARLY EMPTY.

MISTYFOOT LOOKS AFTER THE KITS. I LIKE HER RIGHT AWAY.

THERE YOU GO...I BET YOU'RE TIRED, AREN'T YOU? JUST TUCK RIGHT IN.

I THINK I'VE DONE THE RIGHT THING. THE KITS ARE HALFCLAN, AFTER ALL. MAYBE THIS IS WHERE THEY'VE ALWAYS BELONGED.

TIGERSTAR ISN'T THERE IN MY DREAM THAT NIGHT. THERE'S ONLY THE TINIEST TRACE OF HIS SCENT.

I MISS HIM...I MISS HIM SO MUCH SOMETIMES.

IT'S PAINFULLY OBVIOUS THAT MY DECISION ISN'T A POPULAR ONE.

AND AS IF THE LOOKS I GET AREN'T ENOUGH...

...SOME OF THEM WHISPER LOUDLY ENOUGH FOR ME TO HEAR THE WORDS.

...OUTSIDERS...HOW DO WE KNOW THEY'LL BE LOYAL?

THEY COULD BE BLOODCLAN SPIES!

LUCKILY FOR US, THE SUSPICION ONLY LASTS A LITTLE WHILE. SOON WE START TO SETTLE IN...

...AND IT'S NOT LONG BEFORE I'M INVITED TO GO HUNTING.

AND ALMOST IMMEDIATELY AFTER THAT, LEOPARDSTAR MAKES THE ANNOUNCEMENT TO THE CLAN:

HAWK AND MOTH ARE BECOMING APPRENTICE WARRIORS.

IT'S EXACTLY WHAT I WANTED FOR THEM.

UNTIL YOUR APPRENTICESHIP ENDS, YOU WILL BE CALLED BY YOUR NEW CLAN NAMES.

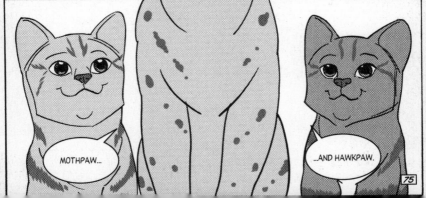

MOTHPAW...

...AND HAWKPAW.

HERE...LIKE THIS. WATCH YOUR POSTURE!

THEIR TRAINING BEGINS AT ONCE. LEARNING HOW TO FIGHT...

...HOW TO HUNT...

...AND HOW TO WATCH AND MAINTAIN THE BORDER OF RIVERCLAN TERRITORY.

THEY EVEN SWIM WELL...WHICH IS CRUCIAL, SINCE SO MUCH OF RIVERCLAN'S DIET IS FISH.

I LIKE TO THINK THE SLEEK FUR THEY GOT FROM ME HELPS A BIT.

BUT THEY HARDLY GET STARTED IN THEIR APPRENTICESHIP BEFORE THINGS HIT A SERIOUS SNAG.

RRRHAAHRR! I'M TIGERSTAR! I'M GONNA TAKE OVER THE FOREST AND KILL EVERYBODY!

NUH-UH! WE'RE GONNA STOP YOU!

GET HIM!

RRHOWR! OH NO, I'VE BEEN GUTTED! LIKE A FISH!

TAKE THAT! AND THAT! AND THAT!

THAT KIT...HE'S PRETENDING TO BE... OUR FATHER...?

WHY'D HE SAY THAT ABOUT KILLIN' EVERYBODY?

WHY'D HE SAY THAT?

I CAN ONLY IMAGINE WHAT EVERYONE THOUGHT WHEN THEY SAW MY KITS.

YOU HAVE TO UNDERSTAND—ALL OF YOU—THAT THAT AREA OF THE CAMP IS ABANDONED FOR A REASON.

WHAT YOU FOUND, CHILDREN, WERE THE REMNANTS OF TIGERSTAR'S HILL OF BONES.

THAT'S WHERE HE FORCED HALFCLAN CATS TO FIGHT EACH OTHER TO THE DEATH.

LEOPARDSTAR EXPLAINS THINGS TO US FOR A LONG TIME. ABOUT HOW MUCH PAIN AND SUFFERING TIGERSTAR HAD CAUSED THEM.

I HAD NO IDEA HE WAS SO CLOSELY INVOLVED WITH RIVERCLAN.

I'M RELIEVED—AND PROUD—THAT NEITHER OF MY KITS MAKES A SOUND WHILE LEOPARDSTAR TELLS US THESE THINGS.

I WAS GOING TO FIGURE OUT SOME REASON NOT TO GO TO THE GATHERING.

I THOUGHT I COULD KEEP THE SECRET OF MY KITS' FATHER AS LONG AS I COULD STAY AWAY FROM SHADOWCLAN.

BUT NOW...

NOW I KNOW WE CAN'T STAY HERE. HAWKPAW AND MOTHPAW ARE TOO VULNERABLE.

I DON'T LOOK FORWARD TO TELLING THEM.

I...HAVE TO TELL YOU BOTH SOMETHING...AND IT'S NOT GOING TO BE EASY TO HEAR.

WE CAN'T STAY IN RIVERCLAN. WE HAVE TO LEAVE, AND GO BACK TO LIVING IN THE WOODS. IT'S NOT SAFE HERE ANYMORE.

NO! NO! I DON'T WANT TO LEAVE! I WANT TO STAY, AND BE A WARRIOR! MAMA—MAMA, DON'T MAKE ME LEAVE...!

MAMA, I CAN'T LEAVE HAWK. I MADE A PROMISE.

IF HE STAYS...I NEED TO STAY, TOO.

WE WON'T MENTION TIGERSTAR'S NAME.

WE WON'T, EVER!

AND...IF WE DON'T TELL.... HOW ELSE WOULD ANY CAT FIND OUT WHO OUR FATHER WAS?

ERIN HUNTER

is inspired by a love of cats and a fascination with the ferocity of the natural world. As well as having great respect for nature in all its forms, Erin enjoys creating rich, mythical explanations for animal behavior. She is also the author of the Seekers series.

Visit the Clans online and play Warriors games at www.warriorcats.com.

For exclusive information on your favorite authors and artists, visit www.authortracker.com.

The #1 national bestselling series, now in manga!

WARRIORS

RAVENPAW'S PATH

SHATTERED PEACE

TOKYOPOP

HARPER COLLINS

ERIN HUNTER

1

KEEP WATCH FOR

WARRIORS

RAVENPAW'S PATH
#1: SHATTERED PEACE

Ravenpaw has settled into life on the farm, away from the forest and Tigerstar's evil eye. He knows that leaving the warrior Clans was the right choice, and he appreciates his quiet days and peaceful nights with his best friend, Barley. But when five rogue cats from Twolegplace come to the barn seeking shelter, Ravenpaw's new life is threatened. He and Barley must try to find a way to overpower the rogues—before they lose their home for good.

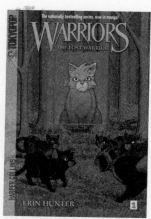

WARRIORS

THE LOST WARRIOR

WARRIOR'S REFUGE

WARRIOR'S RETURN

Find out what really happened to Graystripe when he was captured by Twolegs, and follow him and Millie on their torturous journey through the old forest territory and Twolegplace to find ThunderClan.

TOKYOPOP
The #1 national bestselling series, now in manga!
WARRIORS
THE RISE OF SCOURGE
HARPER COLLINS
ERIN HUNTER

THE RISE OF
SCOURGE

Black-and-white Tiny may be the runt of the litter, but he's also the most curious about what lies beyond the backyard fence. When he crosses paths with some wild cats defending their territory, Tiny is left with scars— and a bitter, deep-seated grudge—that he carries with him back to Twolegplace. As his reputation grows among the strays and loners that live in the dirty brick alleyways, Tiny leaves behind his name, his kittypet past, and everything that was once important to him— except his deadly desire for revenge.

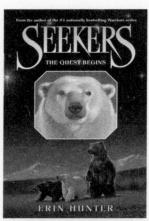

POWER OF THREE

WARRIORS

SUNRISE

ERIN HUNTER

TURN THE PAGE FOR A PEEK AT
THE NEXT WARRIORS NOVEL,

POWER OF THREE

WARRIORS

BOOK 6:
SUNRISE

The secret of Hollyleaf's, Jayfeather's, and Lionblaze's true identities has been revealed, but one shocking question remains unanswered. Now, in the harshest days of leaf-bare, Clanmate turns upon Clanmate, danger lurks behind familiar faces, and one more warrior may be lost forever. . . .

Dead bracken rustled beneath Lionblaze's paws as he stalked through the forest. Above the leafless trees, the sky was dark and empty. Terror raised the hairs on the young warrior's neck, and he shivered from ears to tail-tip. *This is a place that has never known the light of StarClan.*

He padded on, skirting clumps of fern and nosing under bushes, but he found no sight or scent of other cats. *I've had enough of this,* he thought, tugging his tail free from a trailing bramble. Panic sparked in his mind as he stared at the darkness that stretched away between the trees. *What if I never find my way out of here?*

"Looking for me?"

Lionblaze jumped and spun around. "Tigerstar!"

The massive warrior had appeared around the edge of a bramble thicket. His tabby pelt shone with a strange light that reminded Lionblaze of the sickly glow of fungus on dead trees.

"You've missed a lot of training," Tigerstar meowed, padding forward until he stood a tail-length from the

ThunderClan warrior. "You should have come back sooner."

"No, I shouldn't!" Lionblaze blurted out. "I shouldn't have come here at all, and you never should have trained me. Brambleclaw isn't my father! You're not my kin!"

Tigerstar blinked once, but he showed no surprise, not even a flick of his ears. His amber eyes narrowed to slits, and he seemed to be waiting for Lionblaze to say more.

"You . . . you knew!" Lionblaze whispered. The trees seemed to spin around him. *Squirrelflight isn't the only cat who kept secrets!*

"Of course I knew." Tigerstar shrugged. "It's not important. You were willing enough to learn from me, weren't you?"

"But—"

"Blood isn't everything," Tigerstar snarled. His lip curled, showing the glint of sharp fangs. "Just ask Firestar."

Lionblaze felt his neck fur begin to bristle as fury coursed through him. "Firestar's a finer warrior than you ever were."

"Don't forget that he's not your kin, either," Tigerstar hissed softly. "There's no point defending him now."

Lionblaze stared at the dusk-lit warrior. *Does he know who my real father is?* "You knew all along that I wasn't Firestar's kin," he growled. "You let me believe a lie!"

Tigerstar twitched one ear. "So?"

Rage and frustration overwhelmed Lionblaze. Leaping

into the air, he threw himself at Tigerstar and tried to push him over. He battered at the tabby warrior's head and shoulders, his claws unsheathed, tearing out huge clumps of fur. But the red haze of fury that filled his head made him clumsy, unfocused. His blows landed at random, barely scratching Tigerstar's skin.

The huge tabby tom went limp, letting himself drop to one side and hooking one paw around Lionblaze's leg to unbalance him. Lionblaze landed among the bracken with a jolt that drove the breath from his body. A heartbeat later he felt a huge paw clamp down on his shoulders, pinning him to the ground.

"I've taught you better than that, little warrior," Tigerstar taunted him. "You're out of practice."

Taking a deep breath, Lionblaze heaved himself upward. Tigerstar leaped back and crouched a fox-length away, his amber eyes burning. "I'll show you who's out of practice," Lionblaze panted.

He forced his anger down, summoning a cold determination—all the fighting moves he had ever learned were at the tips of his claws. When Tigerstar sprang at him, he was prepared; he dived forward and hurled himself underneath his opponent's belly. As soon as Tigerstar's paws hit the ground, Lionblaze whipped around and landed a couple of blows on the tabby tom's hindquarters before leaping out of range.

Tigerstar spun to face him. "Better," he meowed, mockery still in his voice. "I have mentored you well."

Before Lionblaze could reply, the huge tabby darted toward him, veering aside at the last moment and lashing out with one forepaw as he passed. Lionblaze felt Tigerstar's claws rake along his side, and blood begin trickling out of the scratches. Fear stabbed at him. *What happens if he kills me here? Will I be really dead?*

His mind cleared. Tigerstar was hurtling toward him again. Lionblaze scrambled aside; he aimed a blow, but felt his claws slide harmlessly through the tabby's pelt.

"Too slow," Tigerstar spat. "You'll have to work harder, now you know that prophecy wasn't meant for you. That was for *Firestar's kin*, wasn't it?" Lionblaze knew that the tabby tom was trying to make him too angry to fight. *I won't listen! All I need to do is win this battle!*

He sprang at Tigerstar again, twisting in the air as he had been taught during those long nighttime visits, and landed squarely on the massive tabby's broad shoulders. Digging in with his claws, he stretched forward and sank his teeth into Tigerstar's neck. Tigerstar tried the same trick of going limp and pulling Lionblaze down with him, but this time Lionblaze was ready.

He wriggled out from underneath the heavy body, battering with his hind paws at Tigerstar's exposed stomach fur. "I'm not falling for that trick twice!" he hissed.

Tigerstar struggled to get up, but blood was pouring from a gash in his belly; he stumbled down again, rolling onto his back. Lionblaze planted one forepaw on Tigerstar's chest and held the other, claws extended, against his neck.

The tabby glared up at him; for a heartbeat, fear flashed in his blazing amber eyes. "Do you really think you could kill me?" he growled. "You'd never do it."

"No." Lionblaze sheathed his claws and stepped back. "You're already dead." He turned and stalked away, his pelt still bristling and all his senses alert in case Tigerstar followed and leaped on him again. But there was no sound from the dark warrior, and soon he was left behind among the endless trees.

Lionblaze's mind whirled. He had beaten Tigerstar! *Maybe I do have power after all . . . but how can I, if I'm not one of the Three?* He paused, scarcely seeing the tangling undergrowth and the trees of the dark forest all around him. *Do I want to know who my parents really are?* he wondered. *Does it even matter?* Maybe it was best to let his Clanmates accept him for who they thought he was, so he could go on striving to improve his fighting skills. *I'm already the best fighter in ThunderClan. I know I can be a great warrior.*

"Ashfur is dead," he meowed out loud. "And Squirrelflight won't reveal her secret to any other cats. It would hurt her Clanmates far too much if they knew she'd been lying to them for so long. Why not let everything stay the same?"

Lionblaze woke to the sun on his face. Most of the cats had already left the den; Lionblaze spotted only the gray-and-white pelt of Mousewhisker, who had kept guard over the camp the night before. Lionblaze's jaws stretched in a yawn. "Thank StarClan I wasn't on the dawn patrol," he muttered.

When he tried to get up, every muscle in his body shrieked a protest; he felt as if his body was one huge ache, from his head to his paws. Down one side, his golden tabby fur was matted with blood. *I hope no cat has noticed that!* he thought as he bent his head and began cleaning up his pelt with swift, rhythmic licks. The fight with Tigerstar had been a dream, hadn't it? Lionblaze didn't understand why he should feel just as much pain and exhaustion as if it had really happened. And he had been cut, as if a living warrior had raked his claws across Lionblaze's flank. . . . He tried not to think about it. *It doesn't matter, because I'll never go back to that place,* he told himself. *It's over.*

He felt better after his grooming, with his fur fluffed up to hide the gash in his side. When he finished, he could hear the voices of several cats just outside the den, though not close enough for him to make out what they were saying. Curious, he rose to his paws, arched his back in a delicious stretch, and pushed his way through the branches into the clearing.

Thornclaw was standing a couple of fox-lengths away; Spiderleg sat close by, while Cloudtail paced up and down in front of them, the tip of his white tail twitching. Cloudtail's mate, Brightheart, watched him anxiously from where she sat with Ferncloud, Brackenfur, and Sorreltail. Honeyfern and Berrynose were crouched nearby, their eyes fixed on Thornclaw.

"Ashfur was killed by a WindClan cat!" the golden brown tom was declaring. "It's the only possible answer." A few of his listeners nodded in agreement, though Lionblaze saw others exchanging doubtful glances.

"Firestar said he thought that one of us did it," Honeyfern mewed, sounding nervous to be contradicting a senior warrior.

"Clan leaders have made mistakes before," Cloudtail meowed. "Firestar isn't always right."

"I'm sure none of us would kill Ashfur," Ferncloud added more gently. "Why would we want to? Ashfur had no enemies!"

I wish that was true, Lionblaze thought.

However much he tried to forget, that night of fire and storm was seared into Lionblaze's memory. He could hear the roar of the flames on the cliff top, and could see them licking hungrily around him and his littermates as Ashfur blocked the end of the branch they needed to scramble toward safety. Squirrelflight's confession rang in his ears again: She had told Ashfur that Lionblaze, Hollyleaf, and Jayfeather were not her kits. It was the only way to save their lives, by pretending she did not care what happened to them, but she had handed Ashfur a weapon more terrible than any flaming branch. Lionblaze knew that the gray warrior would have announced the truth to all the Clans at the Gathering; only death had closed his jaws forever and kept the secret safe.

"Lionblaze! Hey, Lionblaze, are you deaf?" Lionblaze

dragged his thoughts back to the hollow to see Spiderleg waving him over with his tail.

"You were Ashfur's last apprentice," the black warrior prompted as Lionblaze padded reluctantly up to the group. "Do you know if he'd quarreled with any cat?"

"Especially any WindClan cat?" Thornclaw added, with a meaningful twitch of his whiskers.

Lionblaze shook his head. "Uh . . . no," he replied awkwardly. He couldn't lie and say that Ashfur had quarreled with a WindClan cat, even though he wished with every hair on his pelt that it was true. Letting his Clanmates believe such a thing could cause an all-out war between ThunderClan and WindClan. "I hadn't seen much of Ashfur just before he died," he added.

To his relief, no other cats questioned him.

"We'd know if Ashfur quarreled with a ThunderClan cat," Brackenfur insisted. "It's impossible to keep a secret around here."

If only you knew! Lionblaze thought.

"Brackenfur's right." Sorreltail touched her nose to her mate's ear. "But all the same, we can't be sure that a Wind-Clan cat—"

"Ashfur died on the WindClan border," Spiderleg interrupted. "What more do you want?"

Sorreltail turned to face him, her neck fur bristling at his scathing tone. "I want a bit more evidence than where his body was found before I start blaming any cat."

Honeyfern and Brackenfur murmured agreement, but

Lionblaze could see that most of the cats were convinced that a WindClan warrior was responsible for Ashfur's death. However much he worried about what that could lead to, he couldn't bury a guilty sense of relief.

"Are we going to let WindClan get away with this?" Thornclaw demanded, his ears lying flat as he dug his claws into the earth.

"No!" Berrynose leaped to his paws. "We have to show them they can't mess with ThunderClan."

Lionblaze's belly churned as he saw the warriors cluster more closely around Thornclaw. They were behaving as if the golden brown tom was their leader, and seemed ready to follow him into battle to avenge their Clanmate's murder.

"It would be best to attack by night," Thornclaw began. "There'll be enough moonlight to see by, and they won't be expecting trouble."

"We'll see they get it, though." Spiderleg lashed his tail.

"We'll head for the WindClan camp," Thornclaw continued. "It'll be best to split up: One raiding party can attack from this direction—"

"What?" The low growl came from just behind Lionblaze. Startled, Lionblaze glanced over his shoulder to see Brambleclaw; he, along with all the other cats, had been so intent on what Thornclaw was planning that he hadn't heard the Clan deputy approach.

ENTER THE WORLD OF

WARRIORS

Warriors

Sinister perils threaten the four warrior Clans. Into the midst of this turmoil comes Rusty, an ordinary housecat, who may just be the bravest of them all.

Warriors: The New Prophecy

Follow the next generation of heroic cats as they set off on a quest to save the Clans from destruction.

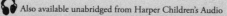 Also available unabridged from Harper Children's Audio

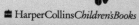 HarperCollins*Children'sBooks*

ENTER THE WORLD OF
WARRIORS

Warriors: Power of Three

Firestar's grandchildren begin their training as warrior cats.
Prophecy foretells that they will hold more power than any cats before them.

Delve Deeper into the Clans

HarperCollins*Children's*Books

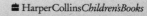